Contents

Computers

Computers are **electronic** machines. They store information and can use the information in different ways.

People use computers at school, at home and at work. ▼

▲ This girl is watching a video on a tablet.

When you think about computers, most people think about **desktop computers** or laptops. However, mobile phones and tablets are computers as well.

Which types of computer do you use most often?

Computer parts

Some desktop computers have two main parts: a **tower** and a **monitor** (screen). The computer is inside the tower. In other desktop computers, the computer is inside the screen.

We use a keyboard to write on a computer. We use a mouse to move and click things on the screen. ▼

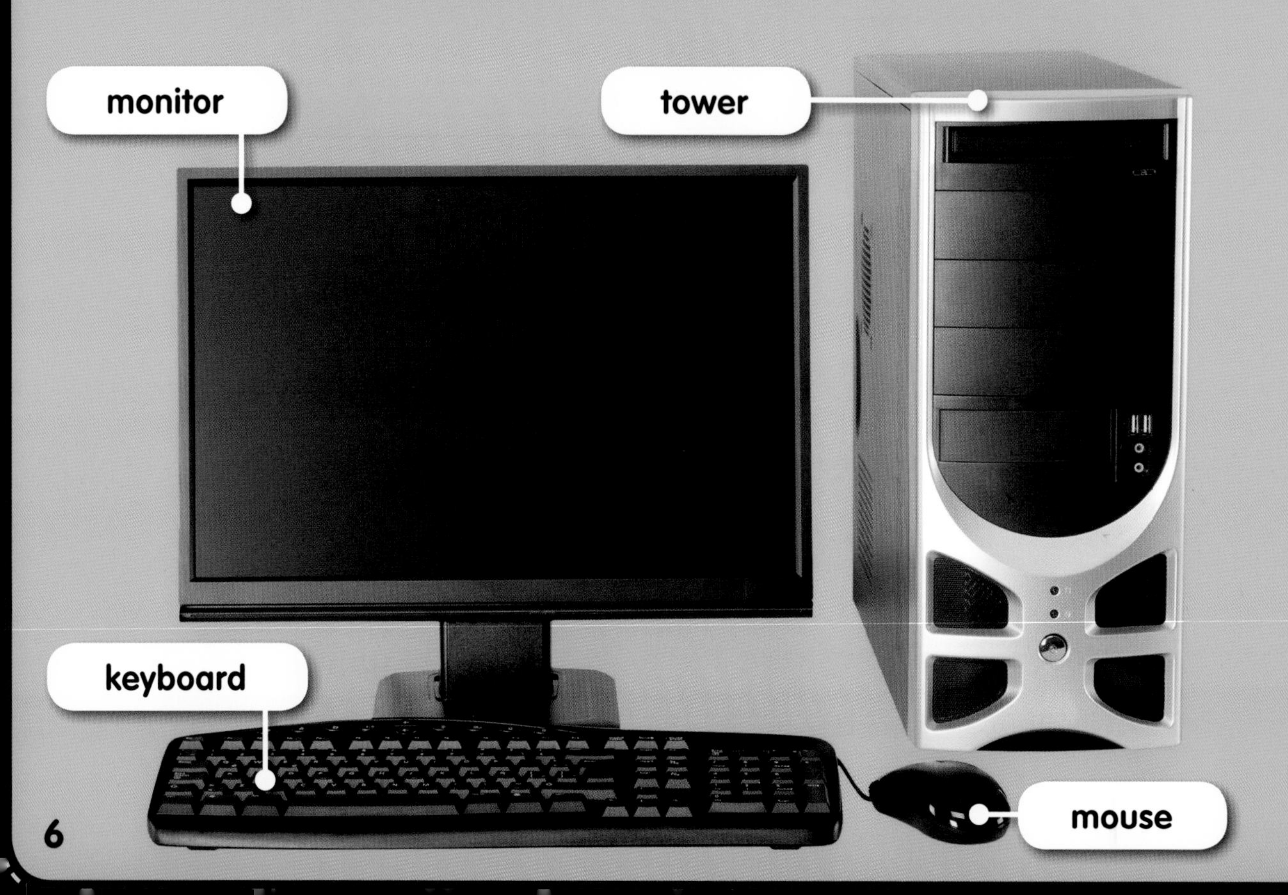

There are many parts inside a computer. They store information and instructions for the computer.

◀ This man has opened a computer tower to fix a problem with the parts inside.

The computer in a laptop is under the keyboard. ▶

Computer programs

A computer program is a set of instructions that a computer follows to perform a task. We use computer programs every day on different **devices**.

▼ **You use a computer program to send a text message on a mobile phone.**

A computer uses different programs for different things. When you type a story or go on the Internet, you are using computer programs.

Video games are powered by computer programs.

Some cars have computer programs that show maps to help drivers find their way.

Can you think of any other devices that use computer programs?

Code

Computer programs are made up of code. It is a special language that tells computers what to do.

Code language is made up of words, letters and symbols. ▼

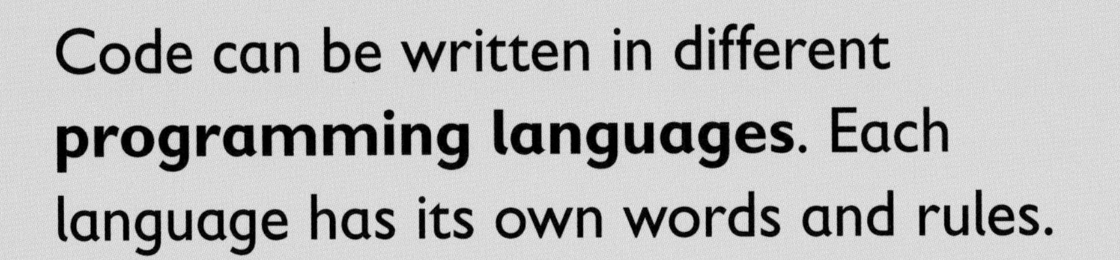

Code can be written in different **programming languages**. Each language has its own words and rules.

▼ **These girls are coding using the Java programming language.**

Do you know any other programming languages?

Learning to code

You can learn to write code. First, you have to choose a programming language to learn. Scratch is a good language for beginners (see pages 14–15).

▲ These children are learning to code at a coding club.

Is there a coding club at your school? If there isn't, you could start one!

When you start to learn how to code, it's best to begin with an easy project. Later, you can do more complicated projects. You can also learn more programming languages.

▲ You can learn how to use code to control robots, such as a robotic arm.

Scratch code

You can learn Scratch code for free on the Internet. The website is scratch.mit.edu.

▼ There are tutorials on the Scratch website to help you understand how it works.

You can use Scratch code to make **animated** videos and games using different **sprites** (characters). You join different coloured blocks of code together to tell the sprites what to do.

▼ **The sprite follows the blocks in order.**

This block says that the animation should begin when you click the green flag.

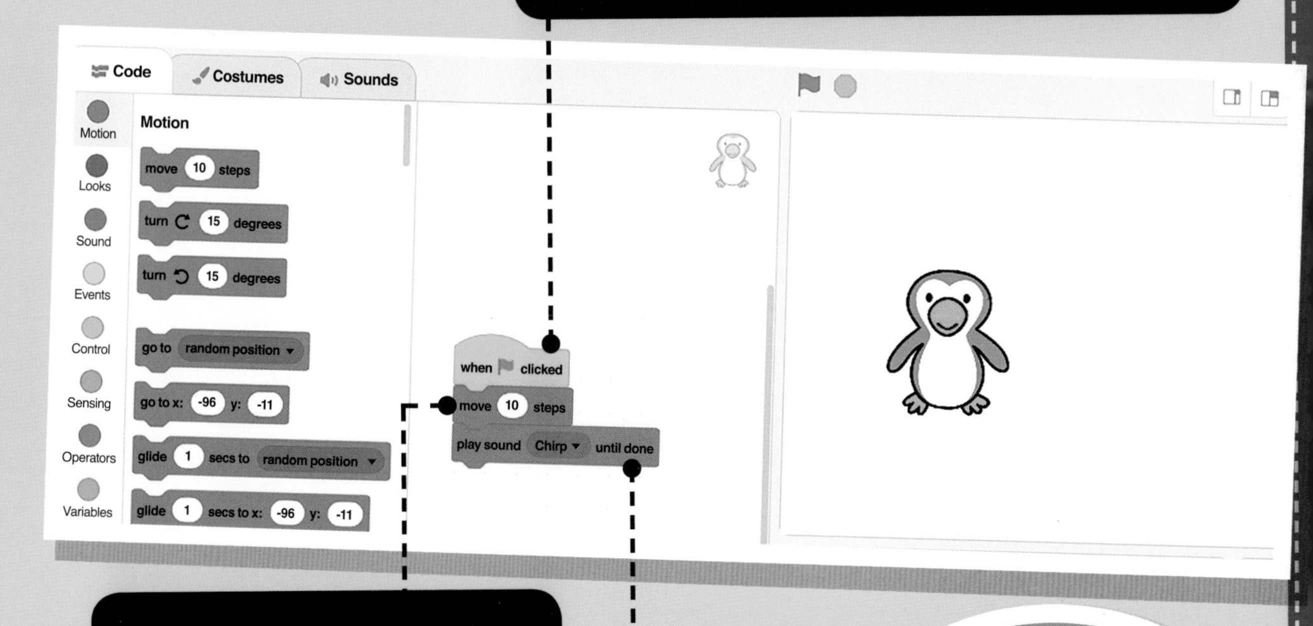

This block says that the penguin should move 10 steps.

This block says that the penguin should make a *'chirp'* sound while it is moving.

If you added a block to tell the penguin to jump after the first yellow block, would the penguin jump or move first?

Websites

Code is used to build websites. People build websites to share information with other people.

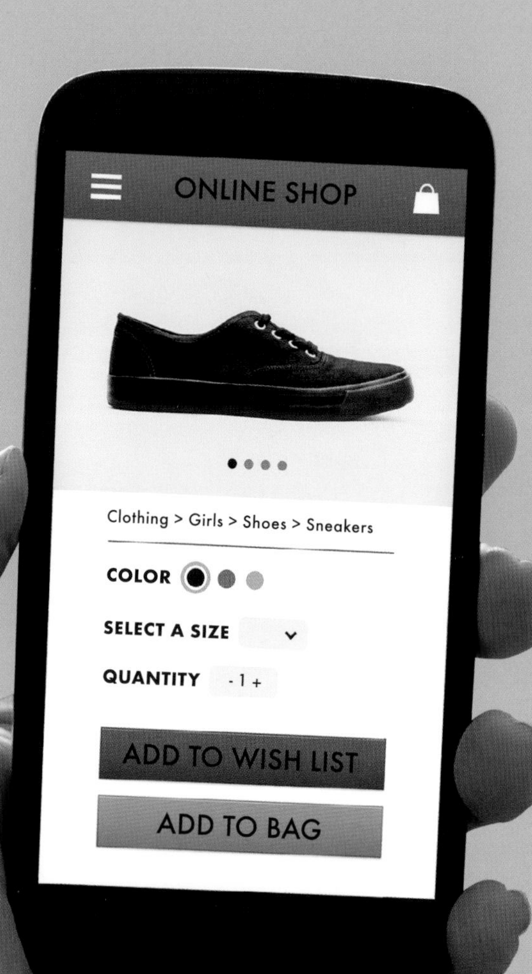

People can buy items online from shop websites. The items are sent to their house in the post. ▶

▲ We can use websites to help with schoolwork or homework.

We look at websites on the Internet to learn information. There are websites with information about science, history, the news and the weather.

Which websites do you look at most often?

Apps and games

Apps (programs) on mobile phones are made from code. We use apps to send messages, go on the Internet and listen to music.

Which apps have you used?

▼ Mobile phones have a calculator app. You can use it to do sums.

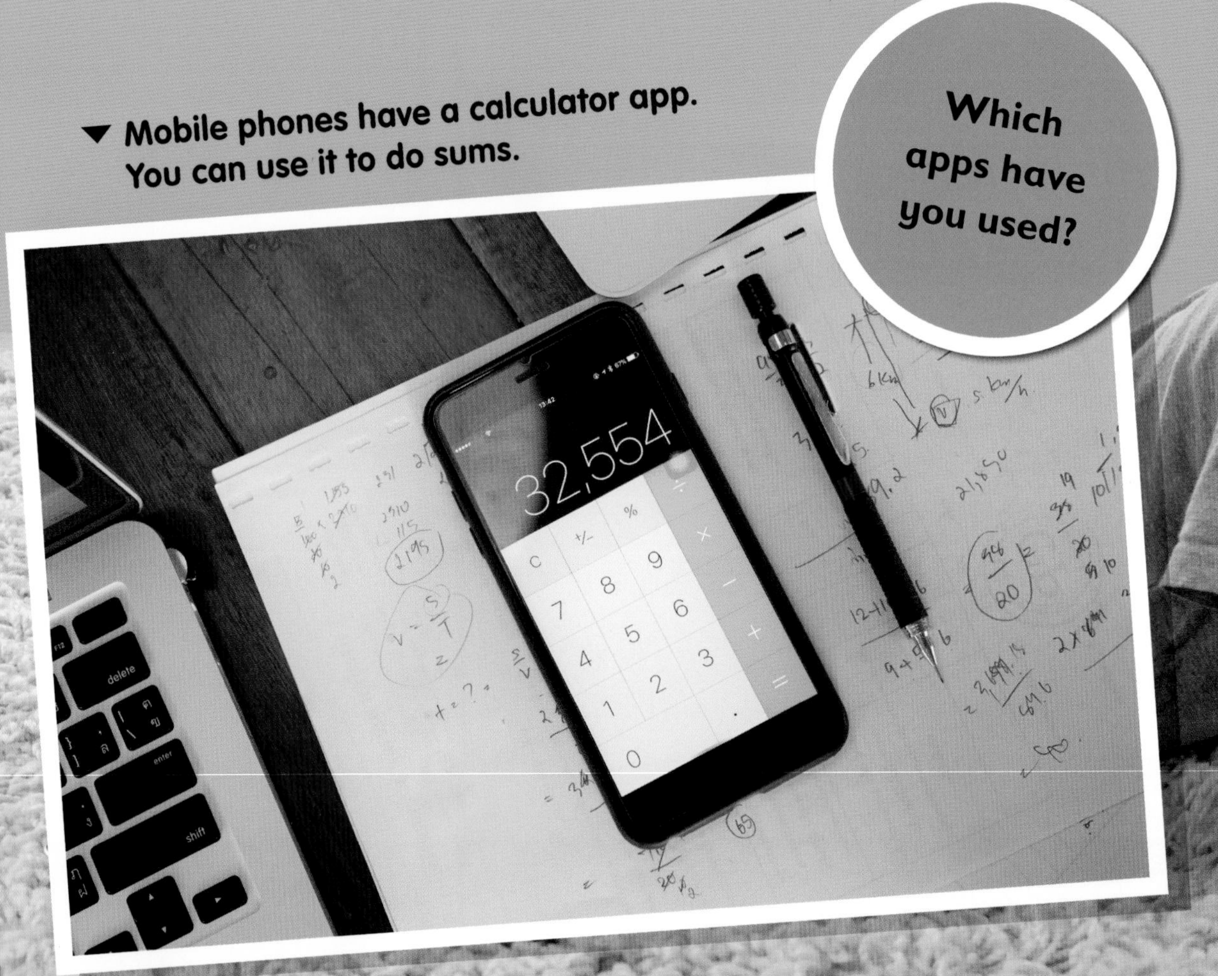

Code is also used to build video games. These games are played on computers, video consoles, TVs, mobile phones and tablets.

Video games are played with controllers or a keyboard. ▼

▼ **On tablets and mobile phones, you touch the screen to play games and use apps.**

Coding jobs

People use coding skills in many different jobs. They use code to make animated films and to record music.

Which job would you like to have when you are older? Would learning code help with that job?

▼ These men are using code to create an animated film.

Scientists make computer programs to help with their **experiments**. Programmers write code to control spacecraft in space and on other planets.

This robot on Mars is controlled by messages written in code and sent from Earth. ▼

Quiz

Test how much you remember.

Check your answers on page 24.

1 Name two examples of computers.

2 What is another name for a computer's monitor?

3 What is a computer program?

4 What is code?

5 What is a sprite in Scratch?

6 How is code used in space?

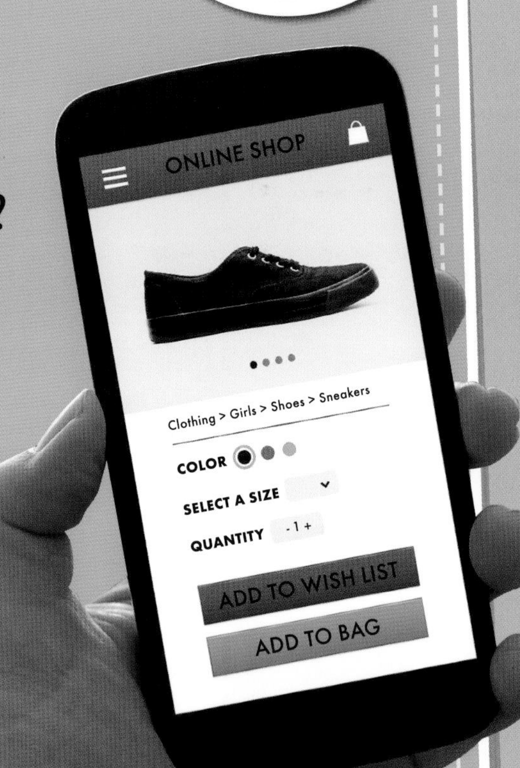

Glossary

animated – describes moving images that are created by a computer

apps – a computer program that is used on a mobile phone or a tablet

controller – a device used to control a machine or program

desktop computer – a computer that has a separate screen and keyboard, unlike a laptop

device – a piece of equipment

electronic – describes a piece of equipment that is powered by electricity

experiment – a test done by scientists

monitor – a computer screen

programming language – a way of writing code that has its own words and rules

sprite – a character in the Scratch programming code

symbol – a sign that is used to represent something

tower – the tall, rectangular part of a computer that contains the main parts

tutorial – instructions that show you how to do something

Index

Answers:

1: Desktop computer, laptop, mobile phone, tablet; 2: The screen; 3: A set of instructions that a computer follows to perform a task; 4: A special language that tells computers what to do; 5: A character; 6: To control spacecraft and robots in space and on other planets

Teaching notes:

Children who are reading Book Band Gold or above should be able to enjoy this book with some independence. Other children will need more support.

Before you share the book:

- What do the children already know about computers? Can you create a class definition of a computer?
- Ask groups of children to make lists of all the computers they know about at home and at school.

While you share the book:

- Help the children to read some of the more unfamiliar words.
- Talk about the questions. Encourage the children to make links between their own experiences and the events described.
- Talk about the pictures. How many different kinds of computers are shown?

After you have shared the book:

- List all the reasons why the people in the book are using computers. How many other reasons for using a computer can the children think of?
- Talk about different jobs that people might do if they can write computer code.
- Work through the free activity sheets at www.hachetteschools.co.uk